MARIE-HÉLÈNE LEBEAULT
AUTHOR OF THE EVERS SERIES

A SUMMER
OF
COURAGE

DEFENDERS OF THE REALM - NOVELLA THREE

BEACHES AND TRAILS
PUBLISHING

ABOUT THE AUTHOR

Marie-Helene Lebeault lives in Quebec, Canada and is the mother of two young adults. A retired teacher, she now spends her days writing, translating academic manuals, and lending her voice to corporate training videos. She enjoys reading, hiking, and going to the beach. She is also an avid rollercoaster fiend and is on a mission to visit all the Six Flags amusement parks with her daughter. Every year, she travels for three weeks on a solo adventure to a new part of the world.

Follow on Social Media, she'd love to hear from you!
www.mhlebeault.com

Also by the Author

The Chronicles of the Starborne Cadets

Stars Beyond Realms

Shadows of Orion

Echoes of the Void

The Nebula's Heart

The Starborne Paradox

Defenders of the Realm

A Journey to Power

The Quest for the Emerald Rattleback

A Summer of Discovery

The Quest for the Sacred Tree

A Summer of Opposites

The Quest for the Phantom Feather

A Summer of Courage

The Quest for the Kraken's Ink

A Summer of Destiny

The Quest for the Cursed Mirrors

The Evers Series

The Ancestors' Key

The Academy

The Time Walker

The World Jumper

Blood Magick Trilogy

The Blood Mage

Blood Magick

Blood Legacy

Standalones

Clarity Castle

What Happens Next?

Ghost Stories

Holiday Shifters

Echoes of Tomorrow

Utopia

Picture Books

Fairy Grandmother: Millie Goes to Antarctica

Fairy Grandmother: Millie Goes to the North Pole

Fairy Grandmother: Millie Goes to China

Fairy Grandmother: Millie Goes to Africa

(Also available in French, Spanish, German, and Italian)

CHAPTER

ONE

THE ELDAVON PALACE was divided into four main sections, each one for a separate branch of government that the four rulers were in charge of.

Herja had never had much interest in living in a palace... which was odd considering that for most of the past four years, she had been determined to be elected as a queen of Eldavon.

She smiled as she walked through the ambassadorial wing, letting her feet follow the twisting, vine-like patterns on the rugs. She had been thirteen when she first decided that, and now at seventeen, she realized it was a much more intensive job than she had expected.

She'd originally wanted it to fix all the problems she saw in the king... and now she knew she wasn't as uniquely brilliant as she once thought.

A nearby door opened, and Herja straightened herself. In plain black trousers and tunic, she was often mistaken for staff by visiting dignitaries, and she had to present a dignified front for Eldavon. She plastered the smile she'd been practicing with Wickham on her face.

To her immense relief, it wasn't a visiting dignitary who left the room but rather the people she had come here to meet. Kaia, Nolen, Icarus and Jalene.

"Herja!" Kaia started when she saw her but rushed to give her friend a hug.

Herja's fake smile turned genuine, and she accepted the hug. "I heard you were back from Odentia—how was your trip?"

"Amazing!" Kaia stepped back and clapped her hands. "Odentia has just the absolutely most beautiful sunsets I've ever seen, and when you walk at night, there're millions upon millions more stars than you see here."

Nolen, Kaia's mate, stepped up beside her. "It was educational, for sure. The new Odentian queen really is the same age as us. And they have a lot of customs different from us, too. It was... kind of intense."

Kaia beamed. "So, what are you doing here at the palace?"

"Wickham's younger twin brothers turned thirteen this year, so they're going to the Silver Springs. Actually, there are over a hundred children making the trip this year." Herja shook her head in amazement. It certainly differed from their year, when it was just over thirty children. "Wick and I have been part of the preparations."

"I thought Donnelly and Rhett were turning thirteen this year. Is Wickham a nervous wreck?"

Herja sighed. He really was, although he was trying to remain reasonable. "He's about what you expect from a big brother with a strong protective instinct."

Kaia nodded wisely. "He is a nervous wreck, then. Well, the four of us were recruited to help pack the children's basic first-aid bags. Do you want to find Wickham and rope him into it as well? It might be good to get his hands busy so he has less time to worry himself to death."

"He was waiting for his family to arrive. They should get in with the next wagon train, and I couldn't get him to do anything else. To quote him, 'Waiting is a full-time job.'" Herja shook her head but smiled—she did understand that, at least a bit. It was difficult to do anything when she was waiting for something to happen.

Nerves smashed in her stomach like icebergs in arctic waters. His family was coming. She had met them during the Winter's feast during the second year of schooling and briefly after she and Wickham were found to be fated mates.

But she was going to have to spend time with them now.

She wasn't ready to meet them. She and Wickham were fated mates, meaning his family would be in her life forever. She wasn't sure she liked that idea, not when she was uncertain about her position in Wick's life.

Even though the orphanage was set up as much like a family as possible, Herja had deliberately stopped herself from seeing them as family. She had spent so long trying to convince herself that she didn't even want a family that she wasn't sure what to do with herself now that she found herself connected to one.

How were families supposed to work? She'd only read about them... and fiction was undoubtedly not reality.

"You guys go ahead," Kaia said as she looped her arm through Herja's. "I need to talk with Herja privately for a moment."

Herja schooled her expression, hiding a grimace, as the others headed off. Kaia led her out of the ambassadorial wing, heading outside rather than deeper into the palace. Once she was sure they were alone, Kaia turned to Herja.

"You need to talk about it?"

Of course, Kaia would pick up on her discomfort. "Wickham's family is incredibly important to him. I'm worried I won't get along with them, damaging our bond."

Not to mention Wickham had confessed to her he had romantic feelings for her. Herja didn't share those feelings—at least, she didn't think she did. And having that discrepancy already put a strain on the two of them.

If she messed things up with his family, it would only make everything all the worse.

"I think you're putting too much pressure on yourself," Kaia offered gently. "Nolan had a terrible first impression with my family, but we all get along now. I think you need just to remember to breathe—this isn't the only time you'll be able to give a good impression."

"But it's the only time I can give a first impression."

"First impressions are overrated." Kaia gave her a soft smile. "Sorry, I know that doesn't help. The only advice I have is to be clear in your communication with Wickham and his family."

Herja frowned at her friend. "In what way?"

"If you're worried about being blunt, say that right away. If you're overwhelmed, tell them. Just be clear and open... and make sure that you don't overexert yourself trying to be what you think they want."

"I do have a problem with understanding people," Herja agreed with a tilt of her head. "So, what do you think they want for their Wickham's mate?"

Kaia squeezed her arm. "They want him to be happy. And he is happy with you, Herja. You're his best friend."

"And that's not less than being a romantic partner," Herja murmured.

"Of course not. It's different, not less than."

Herja managed to smile at her friend. "How can you be so wise when you're the same age as me?"

"Because we're talking about your problems, and it's easy to be wise when you're not the one embroiled in the center of them," Kaia replied with a laugh.

They were drawing closer to the courtyard. Dozens of families had already arrived and had set up tents. It was full of bustling activity but no more chaotic than your average marketplace. Herja's nerves grew all the same.

"Look, Wickham's by the gates," Kaia said, nodding. She released Herja. "He could probably use the company."

Herja managed a small smile. Then she took a deep breath and headed toward Wickham, ready to face her most challenging situation yet: meeting his family.

CHAPTER
TWO

A SMITH BURST over Wickham's face as he saw his mother and father walking alongside the wagon train. They held hands, smiling and laughing, while Donnelly, Rhett, and Tara walked beside them.

Herja drew up beside him, and Wickham seized her hand before he even greeted her.

"They're here!" he exclaimed, pulling her along. "Mother! Father!"

His parents looked ahead and grinned, waving. Wickham waved back, tugging Herja along as he raced to meet them. When they reached each other, there were a lot of hugs and exclamations of welcome.

Herja hung back slightly, not that Wickham expected anything else. This explosion of energy and affection had to be off-putting to her. He caught Tara and hugged her tightly when she raced past him to Herja —at six now, she didn't quite understand personal boundaries.

"You're getting so small," he teased. "Look at you! You're ten feet shorter than when I last saw you."

"No, I'm taller," Tara laughed.

Wickham released her and tickled her sides. "No, shorter."

"Taller!" Tara squealed.

Wickham chuckled as he straightened. Donnelly and Rhett hung back in a reserved demeanor, both with serious expressions. Wickham knew the feeling of wanting to be grown-up and important during this special occasion.

He held his arms out to his brothers. "May I have a hug?"

Rhett came forward readily and gave him a quick side hug, but Donnelly hung back, wrinkling his nose.

"I don't really want to hug right now," he said.

Wickham nodded and lowered his arms again. "You all remember Herja?"

He turned and gestured for her to join him. Herja stepped forward hesitantly, her shoulders straighter than they usually were. The stiffness in her posture made him wince, but then again, it was to be expected. She hadn't ever spent a lot of time in a family setting.

"Of course," Mother said, smiling at Herja. "It's so good to see you again."

"Thank you. You as well. I believe we can set your tent up... I have a map for your designated area," Herja said, reaching into her pocket. Her expression remained stiff.

"That's wonderful, thank you," Father said with a grin. "It's been quite a journey, and we're all ready to have a place to call home for a few days."

Wickham reached for Herja's hand, and she let him take it but kept it so limp that he quickly released her again. He shifted from foot to foot as Herja handed Father the map but remained quiet with that stiff expression on her face.

"Herja and I have been busy," Wickham blurted, not liking the silence. "Herja, tell them how busy we've been."

He lifted his eyebrows at her, hoping she would take the hint and start talking more.

Herja stared back, swallowed, then cleared her throat. "We have been swamped. I apologize if I'm being quiet and awkward. I'm not used to family dynamics, and I find this entire situation extremely nerve-wracking."

The three kids stared at her incredulously, like they didn't understand. Wickham flinched and opened his mouth, but Mother spoke first.

"Oh, honey, we understand. I remember when I met David's parents. I was so nervous I nearly threw up all over them." Mother chuckled. "We've been enjoying the letters you've sent. It feels like we know you already."

Wickham turned to Herja in surprise. "You've been writing letters to my family?"

"Yes. Didn't I tell you that?"

"No."

Herja's cheeks turned red as she ducked her head. Her shoulders curved inward. "Oh. I thought I told you. Yeah, I've been writing. I thought it was a good idea."

"It is. I just guess it's a surprise."

Wickham smiled at her, hoping that he hadn't put her more on edge. It really was a good thing that she was writing to his family. It meant that they had more contact than he was aware of, which would hopefully mean this awkward introduction phase wouldn't last too much longer.

"Well, how about we all look around?" Father said. "Me and the kids have never been here before. What would you suggest we go see first?"

"Probably the fountain," Herja said, tilting her head to one side. She scrunched up her nose as she did when thinking hard.

And Wickham's stomach fluttered. It was just so adorable. He had to quickly avert his eyes for fear of her seeing his attraction to her. Even though she knew his feelings toward her, she didn't share them. He knew she was uncomfortable with it, too, even if she didn't say so.

He didn't blame her. They were tied together as tightly as two people could be. It'd be a long, rough lifetime together if he were pining after her the whole time.

"The ceremonies won't start for a while," he said. "The fountain's a good idea."

"Let's go!" Tara exclaimed.

She bounced forward and seized Herja's hand. Herja stiffened, her eyes flicking to Wickham with a clear 'Help.'

Wickham hurried forward and extracted Tara from Herja. "Hey, boundaries. Herja isn't used to kids, okay? You need to ask before you hold her hand or hug her."

Tara huffed. "Why?"

"Because Herja's not used to kids," Wickham repeated. "And it's polite."

"Herja, can I hold your hand when we look at the fountain?" Tara asked, pouting.

Herja shook her head. "I'm not going to look at the fountain. I have some more things that I need to take care of."

"But you'll be back for the nighttime feast, right?" Wickham asked, his heart dropping.

Herja shook her head again. "I'm going to be busy. But I can join you all for breakfast tomorrow, if that's all right."

Wickham looked at his parents, who were both nodding. He repressed a sigh. After telling Tara to hold back, he couldn't really ask Herja to forgo these mysterious plans and join them, anyway.

"I'll see you later," he said reluctantly.

Herja nodded in answer and walked away. Wickham watched her go—but not for long as Tara clung to him, demanding to go to the fountain. With a smile, Wickham led the way. Herja would get used to the family.

He just had to give her time.

CHAPTER
THREE

HERJA QUICKLY HEADED for the kitchen, trying desperately not to over-analyze every micro detail of what had just happened. Her thoughts lingered on Wickham's question about dinner... was it just a casual mention, or did he want her there? Had he planned something?

She shook her head, trying to push it from her mind. No, she couldn't start trying to figure out the 'hidden details' of Wickham's words. He'd find her and tell her if he had something he needed to say or if the feast was important.

Right? He knew she wasn't great at reading the room...

Ugh. She was going to drive herself crazy if she kept this up! Nope, the best idea was to find something to occupy her hands with. Hopefully, something that would require so much attention that she didn't have time to think, either.

And right now, with everything still being prepared for the children's journey, there was no lack of space to keep busy.

She didn't want to have to field questions from her classmates, so she avoided the first-aid area. Instead, she went to the kitchen. It was hot and sweaty inside, but with so much happening, there had to be something for her to do.

"Hello," she said once she found the volunteer coordinator's table. "I'd like something to do, please."

The coordinator looked at their list and handed Herja a small map. "Go to this storage closet, closet 13b, and find the boxes of napkins. They're labeled 'Silver Springs.'"

Herja checked over the map quickly. It seemed straightforward enough. "Right. And then, do you want me to bring them back here?"

"No, to the laundry," the coordinator replied, handing Herja another map. "There should be wheeled lifts for you in this corner," they marked an X in the storage closet. "Come back when you've delivered the napkins."

"Thank you," Herja said politely.

She headed off, keeping a close eye on the map. The palace was well-designed, but its sheer size made it easy to get lost.

She found the closet quickly enough. When she entered, she found King Lantos sitting on a wooden crate, a handful of note cards in his hands. He bent over them, his brow furrowed.

"Oh," Herja said in surprise.

King Lantos looked up and got to his feet. "Ah, my apologies. I didn't mean to startle you."

"I should be apologizing. You were here first," she said awkwardly.

Herja stepped in, remembered belatedly to curtsy, and headed toward where the lifts should be. There was one left.

"What were you sent for?" King Lantos asked.

Herja bit her lip. Even though she and Wickham had been at the palace for some time now, she had had little to do with the kings and queens. She saw them occasionally but wasn't close to them like Kaia.

Kaia still had regular tea with the former human queen, Charlize. This also meant she often interacted with the other kings and queens, as Charlize still lived at the palace.

"I'm looking for napkins," she finally said. "I'm supposed to take them to the laundry."

"Ah, yes. The Silver Springs napkins. They should be..." King Lantos looked around and pointed at the top of a shelf. "As I suspected. Way at the top."

He pulled a stool over and climbed onto it, despite Herja's protests. Her cheeks warmed thoroughly as the king lifted boxes off the shelf with his silver eyes and intimidating presence and handed them to her to stack on the lift.

"It's fine. I needed a break from my speech anyway," King Lantos said. "After all, I need to make sure it's entertaining enough so that nobody interrupts me."

Herja froze.

She looked up cautiously to see the king's eyes dancing as he attempted to keep a straight face.

"How could you possibly recognize me?" she demanded with a groan. "You see hundreds of different children every year."

"Don't take it personally, I never forget a face," he replied as he brought the last box down.

Herja took it and put it on the lift. "I suppose I should apologize for that. I was quite rude, but you were very kind in your response."

"You weren't the first child to get impatient during the ceremonies, and you won't be last," the king replied, smiling at her. "Of course, your year had many more... events than normal, too. Professor Farrow at the Institute is a good friend of mine. They've told me a bit about you."

"Not too much, I hope," Herja replied guardedly.

King Lantos shook his head. "No. Farrow's good like that; they only say what's important. They're impressed and worried about how you and your friends handled Finnegan last year."

"Worried?" Herja pressed. "Why would they be worried?"

King Lantos arched one of his dark brows at her. "Because you're seventeen and shouldn't be going through all this. Wouldn't you be worried if any of the children in the courtyard were put in a position where they had to take an Odentian warrior prisoner?"

Herja wrinkled her nose. "I don't know. I'm not that great with hypothetical situations."

"Fair enough," the king laughed. "Farrow tells me that you're planning on working your way to being my replacement someday, too."

Herja's blush deepened. She had never thought of it that way, but it was true. If she were to become queen, it would be as the dragon queen. Since Lantos was currently the dragon king, he would have to retire before Herja took the position.

"That's a long way off," Herja muttered, waving her hand. "Besides that, I don't really know that I want to be queen after all. There's a lot more to it than I thought."

King Lantos hummed. "Really? Such as what?"

"You're a king; you'd know better than me," Herja shot back.

"But I don't know what you thought it would be like."

Herja opened her mouth to argue but closed it again. Yes, that was true. She took a moment to collect her thoughts. "I thought it would be more like, I see a problem, tell people how to fix it, and then move on to the next problem. There's a lot more subtlety and... people than I thought."

"There are many people," King Lantos agreed.

"And I'm not great with people. I get awkward and weird, and I just don't know if that means I'd be better off, you know, not being the face of Eldavon." Herja grimaced. "I'd hate to say one wrong thing and cause a war."

"It's not as simple as that," King Lantos said, then shrugged. "But it is challenging. I still feel pretty awkward when dealing with people, too. See?"

He showed her his cue cards. To her surprise, it wasn't a speech written on them but notes on keeping himself calm and exuding a sense of purpose. Herja flipped through them, her frown deepening.

"But you're the king. Why aren't you used to it?"

"Because some things you don't get used to."

Herja handed back the cards. "I don't know why, but you have to be tricking me."

He laughed. "So, you think I made these cards and hid in a closet just to trick you?"

"Why not?" Herja sighed, though she recognized his point. "Apparently, I'm the center of the universe, so..."

Lantos chuckled again. "What does your match think about possibly being a king one day?"

Herja blew out her breath. "We haven't talked about our future.

Besides that, he's in love with me, and I'm not in love with him. But we haven't even talked about that. So I'm unsure of how to talk about the future with him."

Part of her said she shouldn't be telling him this, as it was none of his business. On the other hand, King Lantos had no stakes in her life. He was the epitome of an objective observer.

"Ah, I see. So that's something you need to talk about sooner rather than later," the king said. "Especially as you will graduate soon."

Herja winced and nodded. He was right. They only had two years left and had to figure out what would happen next. She cleared her throat and gestured to the napkins. "I should get this to the laundry. Lots to do."

King Lantos nodded. "Yes, there is. I hope you figure out what you want to do, Herja."

"Thanks," she muttered in return.

Figure out what she wanted to do... and talk to Wickham about their future. She wasn't sure which one was more challenging.

CHAPTER
FOUR

THE NEXT COUPLE of days were a whirlwind of energy. Wickham could hardly keep up with it himself, and while he was disappointed that Herja kept her distance most of the time, he also couldn't blame her. She did make a concentrated effort to spend a little time with his family every day, which was about as much as he could ask for.

The energy levels dropped off suddenly when the children started their journey up Mount Eldavon. They would all be going together, a record number of over a hundred.

And Wickham was left with an excess amount of energy he didn't know what to do with. He tried to spend time with his parents but found they were too chill about it.

Herja found him as he was scrubbing down the cobblestones in the courtyard. Nobody asked him to do this, but he wanted to keep busy.

"You're still worried that Odentia will attack again, aren't you?" she asked as she observed the trail of soapy water behind him.

Wickham looked up guiltily. "Er..."

Herja crouched next to him and tipped over his bucket. "This will not help. Go get a pack with some food, water, and a bedroll. We'll tail them."

"Tail them?" Wickham repeated.

"Yeah. Follow them from a distance to make sure nobody attacks them." Herja's silver eyes locked on him, clear and self-assured.

Wickham leaned back, shaking the excess water from his hands. "Uh... but we need to stay here. The Crown has many protections up, and the mountain is guarded against any attempts."

Herja lifted one brow at him. "Yeah. It is. But you're scrubbing the road."

"It's the courtyard," Wickham protested.

"You're on your hands and knees, scrubbing a footpath. Get your stuff, and I'm not letting you worry yourself to pieces."

She straightened and headed away but paused and looked over her shoulder at him. "I'll tell Kaia and get her to go with me to tell the kings and queens. You tell your parents. Meet you at the base of the path in an hour."

Wickham straightened and grabbed his now-empty bucket. Yeah, maybe it was overkill, but it was better than sitting around worrying, just as Herja said.

He hurried back to his camp, where Mother and Father were talking to the parents of another of the children. They fell silent as he drew up to them.

"Herja and I are going up the mountain," he told them as he looked for his pack.

"Up the mountain?" Mother repeated.

Wickham nodded. "Herja's telling the kings and queens now. We want to monitor the children if Odentia tries anything again."

Father stepped away from the other set of parents, folding his arms. "Wickham. There are plenty of protections up. You shouldn't go. The twins are plenty capable of taking this journey on their own. They've been looking forward to it."

"But I will not interfere. Just in case."

"Wick..." Mother sighed as she shook her head. "They're not little children anymore. And don't tell us this is in case Odentia comes after them. There are far too many protections in place for that to happen again. You're worried in the way you're always worried. Are they eating? Will they stay hydrated? Are they going to be warm enough at night?"

Wickham shoved his blankets into the pack, scowling. Okay, so maybe he was more worried about if they would look after themselves the right way. But it was three days to the top of the mountain and another three days down.

Even though they had rest stops every night, six days were too long for his twin brothers to be alone.

Mother and Father glanced at each other, but neither said anything further. Wickham was grateful because now that Herja had suggested it, he couldn't get it out of his head. He more than wanted to do this— he needed to.

Once he was finished gathering his things together, he went to the trail and waited. The hour was almost up when Herja arrived, bringing a knapsack holding her magical bookbag.

"I have all the food and water we'll need for a week in here," she told him, patting the knapsack. She grinned as though enjoying a private joke. "The kings and queens want me to reassure you that there is nothing to be worried about but said we could go, anyway."

Wickham nodded his relief. After the way Mother and Father had reacted, he worried that the Kings and Queens would tell them they weren't allowed on the mountain.

"Were they upset?" Wickham asked as they started up the trail. They'd keep to the path until they heard the children, then break off into the trees to ensure they weren't spotted.

Herja's forehead creased. "Why would they be upset?"

"I don't know. Maybe they thought I doubted their protections?"

Herja's expression cleared. "No. I explained the situation, and they understood because we're from our year."

Wickham had to wince at that. Yes, the twelve students from their year, six witches and six dragons, certainly had gone through a lot. It seemed like every year they had one big event that took up all their time.

He shook his head. "I hope next year is better."

"Mermaids and krakens... what could go wrong?" Herja asked.

Wickham sighed. *Yeah. That didn't sound very promising.* From what he heard, the fourth year dealing with mermaids caused most students the most trouble. And they had had trouble every year...

He pushed that aside. No use worrying about that. Right now, he had to focus on his mission to ensure his brothers got to and from the Silver Springs safely.

They caught up to the children quickly. They were loud, laughing and chatting and swapping life stories. Wickham and Herja veered off the trail and walked alongside them from a distance, just close enough to hear their laughter but far enough that they couldn't hear them.

"They sound like they're having a good time," Herja mentioned as she used her walking stick to battle through the brush.

Wickham nodded his agreement and slapped a mosquito. "We need some lemongrass. I hope Rhett and Donnelly remember it. I showed them how to find it, but they don't always think about putting it on, even when the mosquitos are terrible."

Herja used her stick to push a branch out of the way and gestured for him to go on ahead. "I'm sure they remember."

"I'm glad the whole family could come to send the twins up the mountain," Wickham continued, compelled to fill the quiet between them. "When it was my turn to come up the mountain, it just wouldn't work, not when Tara was so young."

"It was strange that only your mother came then, but everyone is here this time." Herja was quickly at his side again. "Can I ask you a question that might be rude?"

Wickham nodded.

"Well... don't you feel a bit upset your parents made an effort for the twins, but not you? Even though Tara was younger, she could still travel. Right?"

Wickham considered what she was saying and shook his head. "I don't see it that way. It's several weeks' worth of traveling, and we were also in different circumstances. We'd just moved, Mother and Father were new at their jobs, and not only was Tara only three, but Rhett and Donnelly were young, too."

"Does that make a difference? Couldn't they have gotten a sitter or a relative to stay with them so your parents could be here?" Herja pressed, looking doubtful.

"Maybe, but like I said, a lot was happening." Wickham frowned at Herja. Why did it feel like she was being judgmental of his family?

Herja shrugged. "Maybe. But your father was sick, too, wasn't he?"

"Yeah. So even if they could arrange childcare—"

"Why wouldn't they tell you beforehand, though?"

"He wasn't sick before we left. Or at least, we didn't know he was. He was just tired a lot," Wickham said defensively.

Herja fell silent, though why he wasn't sure—was it his tone or something else?

His heart sank. Did this mean she didn't like his family?

CHAPTER

FIVE

HERJA ROLLED her shoulders and bent to the side, releasing the tension in her lower back. The children had kept up a pretty good pace, which on top of hurrying to catch up, had caused her muscles to seize up now that they were resting.

Wickham was stretching out his legs, his eyes shut.

"You doing all right?" Herja asked him.

Wick didn't do great with steep inclines. They'd been working on increasing his stamina since last year saw them running all over a mountain, but again rushing to catch up to the children and then blazing a trail through rough terrain wasn't helpful.

"I'll be fine," he told her, though he sounded tired. "I just think I over-packed."

"We can put your pack into the bookbag," Herja offered, wincing. There was still plenty of room in there, and with the magic on it, the weight of his pack would be negligent in comparison.

She reached for the back when a shout broke through the forest.

"Help, help!"

Wickham's eyes snapped open. He was on his feet instantly, leaving their packs behind as he raced for the sound.

Herja jumped in surprise, grabbed her sack and his pack, and grunted under the weight of it. What did he have in here, bricks?

She pulled it over her shoulders, wedging it over her own, and headed after him. She caught up with him just before they reached the sound of the cries for help and grabbed his arm to pull him to a stop.

"That's Donnelly's voice," Wickham told her, shaking.

Herja nodded. She suspected it was one of his brothers. "We have to approach carefully. We don't want to ruin the trip if he really doesn't need help."

Wickham opened his mouth, looking stressed, but nodded.

They moved forward again, with Herja making sure she took the lead. She dropped the packs when they were closer and gestured to Wickham to crouch. Though her training in moving through mountainous terrain was more inclusive than his, he still moved silently behind her.

Soon, they found Donnelly. He stood in the middle of bramble bushes, the thorns having caught his clothes. A few tears streaked down his face.

Wickham started forward, but Herja caught him.

"He needs me," Wickham whispered.

"No, he doesn't. He's not bleeding, and he isn't stuck. He can get himself out of this," Herja replied.

Wickham shot her a look that told her he wasn't happy but crouched near her.

Donnelly wiped his eyes. "Help," he called, but he seemed annoyed now rather than sounding hurt or afraid.

Wickham, however, looked like even this cry was enough to make him want to run up into the clearing and rescue his brother... even though Donnelly didn't need to be saved.

"Just wait," Herja advised as he stood straighter.

Wickham gave her an angry look that nearly changed her mind, but Herja bit her lips together and focused instead on Donnelly. He could get out of this himself and would be better off knowing that he could get himself out of scrapes.

Donnelly growled and quickly picked his clothes out of the bramble, freeing himself within seconds. Once out, he looked down at himself, then back up. A grin burst over his face as he took off back toward the path.

"Hey, guys!" he yelled at the top of his lungs. "I'm okay!"

Wickham sat back on his heels, letting out a deep breath. He ran a hand through his silver hair.

"You're shaking," Herja said in surprise.

Wickham swallowed. "Yeah... I'm sorry."

"For what?" Herja mumbled, straightening.

"For that look I gave you. You were right."

Herja sighed. "They're thirteen. They're getting old enough that they need to resolve their own issues unless they're too big. You saw how easily he freed himself. I know I can't talk about what it's like to be an older sibling, but I really do think children should be encouraged to have independence."

Not that she knew much about children at all. She had spent her own childhood trying very hard not to be one.

The rest of the day went by without incident, and when the children came to the first set of cabins, Wickham and Herja found a lovely spot next to a brook to set up their own camp. Herja found herself enjoying the peaceful, quick way they helped each other set up their tents, then set a fire and started cooking. There was a domesticity to it even here in the woods she enjoyed.

As darkness fell around them, Herja fingered the band of silvery threads she had woven into a bracelet. Wickham also wore one—their star threads, which bound them together.

She was reminded about what King Lantos had said to her and bit back a sigh. "Wick?"

"Hmmm?"

"We're going to graduate in a couple of years... have you thought about what the future is going to look like for us?"

Wickham looked up from the fire. "I want to go to medical school. Which school depends on you. And what you're planning."

Herja shivered slightly. It seemed too powerful a position to hold Wickham's future in her hands like that.

"I'm glad you brought it up," Wickham continued as he looked back at the fire. "Because I don't really know what you want... what you're planning."

"I don't really know what I'm planning, either." Herja admitted.

Wickham's brow puckered as he nodded, encouraging her to continue.

"Everything seems in flux. I have never really doubted what I was going to do, but now I realize that if I still want to be a queen, I need to have a reason for it. A specific purpose that I'm working toward. And I just don't know what that will be."

"You have a lot of good qualities," Wickham said.

"Yes, but between deciding to pursue a diagnosis only to have 'inconclusive' results again and again and now wanting to be adopted... it just feels like I have nothing to hold on to," she admitted.

Except for Wickham. And the problem with that was that she realized she did want romance in her life. When she read over the bits of her novel she wrote, she realized she was writing a heroic version of herself trying to find love.

She didn't know what romance meant to her... and was worried that it would end with her pushing Wickham away someday.

"You have me," Wickham told her, moving closer. "I'll always be here for you to hold on to."

She gave him a distracted sort of smile. Yes, he would always be here for her... until he found someone more important to him. She felt guilty even thinking about it, but she couldn't help all these doubts that made it hard to think.

Wickham moved away again. "Is this about when I revealed I had feelings for you?"

Herja flinched, unable to stop herself.

"So, it is." Wickham turned his face away and ran a hand through his hair again.

"It's not that simple," Herja said.

"Herja... I know it's a lot of pressure on you, even though I don't mean to put it on you." Wickham looked up through his lashes, seeming hesitant. "If you want, we can agree to date other people. Maybe that will relieve some of the pressure from our relationship."

Herja bit her lips together. "Is that what you want?"

"I want you to be happy. And if that means I need to be more active about getting over my crush on you, then...." Wickham shrugged, not looking at her. "Maybe it will make us both feel less like we have this invisible wall between us."

Herja's instinct was to say no; she didn't want that—but why not? She closed her eyes, trying to picture herself holding hands and maybe even kissing someone. None of the faces she brought to mind felt right.

Then she imagined it was Wickham, and warmth filled her chest.

Her heart started to pound, and she opened her eyes quickly. "I don't want to talk about that."

It wasn't fair to Wickham to get his hopes up when she wasn't sure.

Wickham looked startled but nodded.

"I can't figure out my future until I've got my past squared away. I asked Row to help me get adopted," she said, babbling now so she didn't have to overthink.

"I know. You told me."

"But I want them to adopt me."

Wickham's eyes widened. "Have you told them that?"

"No. It just doesn't seem right to ask something like that." She frowned at the fire. "Ugh. Never mind. I'm not making any sense."

Wickham sighed. "You don't like to be vulnerable. That makes total sense."

Herja didn't reply. Because he was right... but admitting it? It made her feel too vulnerable.

CHAPTER
SIX

WICKHAM WOKE up early the following day and started breakfast while Herja slept. A grey sky greeted them, and he looked worriedly at the clouds. Was this a harbinger of rain? Did the children have supplies to protect them if it thundered?

When he shared his worries with Herja, she nodded. "Yes, they have supplies. Remember when we came up? We were given rain ponchos."

"But what if—"

"Wick." Herja laid her hand gently on his, silencing him. "They're as prepared as we were."

It was a little comforting because when they had made their journey, at least nothing too terrible had happened on the way up. They finished their breakfast and cleaned the camp, leaving nothing behind.

When they resumed their watch, the children were already on their way, laughing and talking again. A few pretended to be dragons, the story they would have heard last night.

After their first break, Herja grew concerned. "That girl who said she was napping isn't with them."

Wickham scanned the crowd of children hidden at the top of a tree. "Maybe she moved on ahead when you weren't looking."

"No, they've left her behind. We should hang back and make sure she's okay."

But that would mean letting his brothers go on ahead with no one to watch them.

"Rhett and Donnelly are up there," he said, pointing.

"But they aren't the ones that need us."

"But they're my brothers."

Herja looked at the sky as though looking for answers. "Wick... remember in our first year? You realized that sometimes, some people need your help more than your family. Helping the child who is actually lost instead of your brothers doesn't mean you don't love them."

Wickham looked back up the path, worrying his lip between his teeth.

"This child does need help," Herja continued. "Your brothers don't."

But that wasn't true. They did need him. He was their big brother; he couldn't just leave them when there was potential trouble!

On the other hand, the child left behind would be upset, and making this journey on their own would be more complicated than in a group. They risked going the wrong way, wandering off the path, and getting lost. The mountain was safe, but this journey wasn't meant to be undertaken alone.

Thinking about leaving his brothers to care for a child he didn't even know made Wickham's heart hurt. He knew what they needed to do, yes, but he hadn't done this for all the children... only Rhett and Donnelly.

"What do you suggest we do?" Wickham asked, stress leaking into his tone. "Just ignore the rest of the children to look after one of them?"

Herja narrowed her eyes like she wanted to tell him yes. "I'm going to keep an eye on the lost child. You can do whatever feels best to you."

That didn't sound like a good idea, either. Wickham groaned as Herja started up the mountain. How were they supposed to learn how to work together when something as simple as this resulted in them going in two different directions?

But we have opposite ideas here. There's no compromise to be had.

Or was there? Wickham rushed after Herja. "Wait!"

She stopped and looked at him, arching one eyebrow. Her entire stance was tense like she was preparing for a fight.

"What if we slow the group down? Then the girl could catch up with them, and it will give them an extra hurdle to overcome on their own?" he suggested, gibbering.

It seemed backward to suggest that they inconvenience the children further, but this would help the girl catch up while Wickham could stay near his brothers.

Herja considered, then nodded. "We go up a hundred meters and slow them down. If they pass us without her catching up, I'm staying with her."

Wickham nodded his agreement.

They started off again, and Wickham had to admit that he was pleased with how he resolved the issue... if only it were that easy to resolve all their problems! And some things just seemed even more impossible to resolve...

Which they would address later. Right now, they had work to do.

Approximately a hundred meters up the mountainside, a footbridge passed over a creek just wide and deep enough that they'd have to swim without the bridge. As Wickham puzzled over how to block the bridge without damaging it, Herja called him over.

"Help me push this old dead tree down," she said.

She didn't need his help, not when she could become a dragon, but Wickham appreciated her including him. The tree was pretty sturdy, so Wickham used a spell to take a notch of wood from the base like they learned in the Golden Forest. From there, Herja could easily knock the tree down, blocking the bridge.

"You think that'll be enough?" Wickham asked as they retreated once more.

"Hope so."

They found a good spot close enough to the road so they could see and scaled a tree, where Wickham then cast a spell to make them both invisible to the road below. As they waited for the children to arrive, Herja kept changing her position.

"What is it?" Wickham finally asked.

"I just keep thinking that the Crown should have divided the children into smaller groups. One hundred is an awful lot to keep organized... not to mention it's really easy for them to slip through the cracks this way." Her brow puckered in how Wickham understood meant she was thinking about something else.

He hesitated, then decided there was no point in pussyfooting around. "You're thinking about how you don't seem to fit in a diagnosis, right?"

Herja's lips thinned as she glanced at him. So, he was right.

"When we get to the top of the mountain, we can ask the Headmasters about it," he offered.

Herja nodded. She looked like she might want to say something more, but the first sounds of the children were heralding their approach. The two tree-bound teens hunkered down and fell silent.

The first children fell silent as they came to the log blocking their way over the footbridge. As more and more started crowding at them, they complained.

"How are we going to get across?" a boy complained.

To Wickham's surprise, it was Rhett who pushed his way to the front and started hauling on it. "Let's just move it out of the way!"

"Right," Donnelly said, striding forward. "Michaela, Heather, John, Bram, you all help Rhett. Amos, Maura, Seth, Rachel, you help me on this end."

Wickham and Herja glanced at each other. Something glimmered in Herja's eyes—pride, perhaps? Was she proud that his brothers easily took charge to resolve the problem?

The log was out of their way in minutes, and the children congratulated each other as they started over. Donnelly stayed behind at the bridge, counting heads as they passed while Rhett inspected the tree. By the time the last child crossed, the girl that had been left behind rejoined them. Tears stained her cheeks, but she didn't seem bothered anymore.

"That's everybody," Donnelly declared as he and Rhett fell in line behind them.

"That tree was knocked over on purpose," Rhett said. "I saw it—a big chunk was cut out."

Wickham swallowed hard. Oops!

Donnelly looked nervously around them. "We better get some big heavy sticks to defend ourselves. Maybe it's the villains that went after Wick."

"Oh, no," Herja murmured.

She and Wickham glanced at each other, wincing—had they just made a terrible mistake?

CHAPTER
SEVEN

THE CHILDREN SPENT the rest of the day preparing themselves to catch the 'bad guys.' Herja was mildly impressed with everything they came up with, although she couldn't get too impressed—after all, their actions proved they were worried and scared.

Just like she had been in their second year, when the adults all thought it was a good idea to continue like normal, despite everything the students had been through. Herja understood a bit better now... after all, she hadn't thought about what effect all the events that had happened these last three years would have affected the children coming into their magic.

In the end, when the children were close enough to the second-night cabins to know that none of them would be left behind, Herja ran ahead to tell the adults stationed there what happened.

"We didn't think they'd realize it was shoved over on purpose," she finished. "I'm not sure if we need to tell them it was us or not, though."

The person she had spoken with, Lori, shook her head. "We'll take care of it and soothe their fears. But you and Wickham should go back to the palace—we have this covered."

Herja had to admit that part of her agreed. So far, they hadn't really done anything that would help the children, after all.

When she brought it up to Wickham, though, he stubbornly shook his head. "Not until they're all safely back as well."

"But why?" Herja asked, shaking her head. "We don't know what we're doing. The adults do. And so far, we haven't really helped much, have we?"

"We made it so that little girl could catch up," Wickham argued. He put his hands on his hips and narrowed his eyes.

He so rarely became this stubborn that Herja was honestly taken aback. She pondered momentarily before asking, "Do you really think Odentia will cause trouble, or are you just hovering?"

"I'm worried for my brothers," Wickham said. He dropped his pack to the ground and picked up twigs and branches, throwing them into a pile for the fire.

Herja silently joined him. It really wasn't her place to question the wisdom of the situation, after all. She didn't understand family dynamics. She didn't know what it was like to have siblings... but if Wickham felt half as protective of them as she felt toward him and their friends, she understood why this was so difficult for him.

Once their fire was set, Herja cooked them some supper. Wickham wanted to do it, but Herja needed something to do with her hands.

"I want to talk about romance," she finally said. As much as the situation with Wickham's brothers ate at her, this was likewise major.

Wickham swallowed and shifted on the spot. "Er... we don't have to. There's no rush in talking about it."

Herja stirred their rice-onion soup and frowned. "Does that mean you don't want to talk about it?"

"Um... well, no, not exactly. I just don't want you to think there's pressure. I don't want to push you away," Wickham continued, clearly struggling between carefully picking his words and blurting it all out.

Herja placed the lid back onto the pot and wrapped her arms around her middle. "Except I just said I want to talk about it. We don't have to if you don't want to, but I want to."

"Are you sure?"

"Yes." Herja took a deep breath, trying to think of the right words to convey her feelings. "I feel like having this sitting between us with no resolutions in sight is putting more distance between us. It's making things feel weird, and I don't know what to do... I'm not sure how to say what I want to say."

Wickham's shoulders were hunched inward. It was clear what he thought she was getting at, but that was just the problem... she wasn't sure what she was getting at.

Or rather, she knew, but she didn't know how to say it.

Finally, she sighed. "I do love you, Wick. I care about you deeply. I just don't know... I don't know what love really is. And what makes the love between best friends different from the love between lovers?"

"I... I guess I don't really know what you're saying," Wickham mumbled.

"I know. So, I'll try to be clearer. I want to have a romantic relationship. The sort where we hold hands and giggle and even share little kisses occasionally." Her cheeks bloomed with heat, embarrassed to be admitting it aloud. "I think I've been wanting this for a while."

Wickham looked up, his eyes wide and hopeful.

Herja bit her lip, knowing her following words had the power to dash that hopeful look on the rocks. "The thing is, I'm not sure if I'm ready for it."

As expected, his shoulders slumped again. "It's okay. If you're not ready, I'll wait."

"But I don't want to wait. I'm terrified of these feelings; I've never felt this way before; I don't really know what it is... but I don't want to wait. I'm so tired of seeing how everyone else looks so happy with their mate, and I'm holding you at arm's length."

Herja ran a hand through her hair, aggravated. Even her thoughts were contradictory; how was she supposed to expect that Wickham would understand what she was getting at?

"I understand your frustration," Wickham said slowly. "But I also think that we need to make sure that we're not just jumping into something because of what we're seeing other people do."

Herja stirred their food again, pondering his words. He was entirely right—they couldn't rush into romance if either of them weren't sure what they felt, which meant she was holding them back.

Back from what, though? If she were sure this would be the happiest thing ever, why would she hesitate?

"I don't know what to do with my feelings. I'm worried that one day I'll wake up, and they'll be gone. Then you'll be hurt, and I don't want that."

"Oh."

Herja peeked up at him. "Oh? Is that everything?"

"I'm thinking." Wickham toyed with the end of his silver braid. "I just don't want you to feel pressured... you're not obligated to feel a certain way for me."

"But what I'm afraid of is misunderstanding my feelings. That's not pressure; that's just me." Herja took another deep breath. "For that matter... we're fated mates. I've said for three years that I want to become a queen. Do you want to be a king?"

Wickham winced.

"I didn't think so," Herja said dryly.

"I've never really thought about it," Wickham admitted.

Herja took the food off the fire, and Wickham started to dish it into two bowls. "It's not unheard of for a king or queen to be solely elected. You don't have to be a ruler even if I am... although I'm not certain that's a good idea."

"Because of me?" Wickham asked quietly.

"Because of a lot of reasons."

Wickham handed her a bowl. "I see... well, when I'm going to medical school; you can always take internships or other things to help you sort it out better. I mean, we don't have to be joined at the hip."

"I suppose not," Herja replied doubtfully.

She started eating, uncertain where else to go with this conversation. She had told him about her feelings. He hadn't exactly responded as she expected... but she also didn't know what she had expected.

She bit back a sigh. Why did emotion have to be so darn complicated?

CHAPTER
EIGHT

WICKHAM SLEPT LITTLE THAT NIGHT; his thoughts filled with what Herja had said. He wasn't entirely sure if she was telling him she loved him in the romantic sense or if she was saying she just wanted to... It was highly confusing, but he didn't want to wake her up to demand more answers.

"Did you sleep at all last night?" Herja asked the following day. She looked as exhausted as he felt.

"Not really," he admitted.

Herja bit her lip, her expression uncharacteristically nervous. "I messed this up somehow, didn't I?"

Wickham shook his head. "Not at all. It's just a lot to think about, you know?"

"All right," Herja replied, her voice small.

"Maybe we can talk about it more tonight?" Wickham suggested.

"Maybe. Let's see how hard the day is first."

Wickham wasn't sure if that meant she didn't want to talk about it at all—but decided he needed to take her at her word in this case. Herja rarely told soft lies. She was generally more straightforward than that.

The morning started off strong, but around mid-morning,

Wickham heard the plaintive sounds of a creature in distress. He hesitated to bring it up, not wanting to get too far from his brothers.

But the children were taking a break, so he told Herja what he heard. They investigated to find a handful of tiny, fluffy creatures. Fuzzy back ends morphed into fluffy front ends. Plumed tails swished, and sharp beaks clacked.

Griffins. Their downy front halves that of eagle chicks, and their furry back halves are lion cubs. Only they were smaller than any lion— these little chick/cubs were small enough that Wickham thought they could each fit in the palm of his hand.

"Look, one of them is hurt," he pointed out. An extended cut ran along the little griffin's flank, red and puffy at the edges. Even from this distance, Wickham knew it had to be infected. "I don't think it'll make it without some sort of treatment."

"The parents are probably around somewhere," Herja said, looking at the sky.

"I know." Wickham crept a little closer. The griffins huddled together, chirping as they stared at him with enormous eyes. They didn't seem to be overly afraid, however.

Griffins were a docile species, even the wild ones like this. These had to have a lot of interaction with people, too.

"We could report it when we go down," Wickham said doubtfully.

"Or you can just try to treat its injury now—I can tell you want to," Herja replied.

Wickham hesitated. He didn't have training to deal with wild animals... but the little thing was obviously bad. How could they be sure veterinarians could find it again if they left?

He moved slowly, inching forward a little at the time. The griffins bobbed their heads and huddled tighter together. It seemed like a good sign—

He picked up the injured one, and it let out a loud screech that hurt his ears. Instantly, there were twin echoing screeches. The griffin struggled in his hands as the others scattered.

Wickham hurried to Herja's side. She took her dragon form, folding her wings over him. The little griffin continued to shriek as Wickham held it in one arm. Bursts of sound batting against Herja's wings told him that the parents were here and trying to get through. Herja shook her glimmering body, growling slightly in pain.

No time to waste. He quickly cleaned out the injury on the griffin's side. Luckily, it wasn't as bad as it first appeared. Once that was done, he gently put on a little honey, which would help prevent further infection. Then wrapped it in bandages he had previously soaked in a pain-killing mixture and secured the bandages with some resin that would gradually work itself free.

He released the griffin, and it scampered through Herja's wings. He grabbed their things, and Herja retook her natural form.

Seizing her hand, Wickham charged through the trees, not caring where they went. Scratches and bruises already covered Herja's face and arms, and with the griffins continuing to dive-bomb them, his only thought was to get them out of harm's way.

Moments later, they stumbled onto the well-worn main path that led up the mountain. The two adult griffins finally turned back, no doubt to check on their young.

"We're going to have to clean those out," Wickham mumbled as he took in the multitude of scratches on Herja's skin. None of them looked deep, but the drops of blood welling up to darken her black clothes made his stomach squeeze.

Her injuries were because of him. He'd been so single-focused that he hadn't even thought about what Herja was going through to keep the griffins off him.

"I'm fine," Herja said, slicking her black hair back. "But we need to—"

Even as she started forward, there was a sudden snap in the forest. A rushing noise like a rope being dragged over wood met Wickham's ears. He turned his head, but too late—a net crashed down on him and Herja, weighted at the edges with logs and rocks.

Within moments, they were hopelessly tangled.

Dozens of children burst from the other side of the forest, opposite the direction where Herja and Wickham had been fleeing the griffins.

"We caught them!" one child crowed. "We caught the villains!"

This girl planted herself in front of the two, brandishing a stick that would no doubt hurt if used to whack them.

"What are you after, villains?" she boomed, poking at them with her stick.

"We're not villains," Herja said, swatting at the stick.

The girl poked them again. "Answer my questions or face the consequences!"

Wickham could hear Donnelly and Rhett approaching amid the chatter. Oh, no! They weren't supposed to know he was here. But even as his mind churned, trying to figure out how to escape without them seeing, Herja snorted.

"I can prove we're not villains," Herja said.

He felt the coolness of her scales before he was aware she was changing forms. In a flash of light, her dragon form replaced her natural state. Her scales slid from royal blue along her belly, turning to amethyst on her sides, and finally emerald green along her back. The children shrank back, gasping.

Herja shrugged the net off her wings as Wickham got to his feet.

But this time, Rhett and Donnelly were at the front of the crowd. Their jaws dropped open as Herja retook her natural form.

"What are you doing here?" they demanded in unison.

The girl with the stick glared at Wickham. "You know these villains?"

Rhett snorted as he turned to her. "They're not villains—that's our brother and his mate."

"Why are you here?" Donnelly demanded.

Wickham opened his mouth, but nothing came out.

"You were checking up on us," Rhett accused. He stomped toward Wickham. "You think we're babies that can't do this on our own, don't you?"

"That's not it at all," Wickham protested.

"Then what is it?" Donnelly yelled.

Herja stepped forward. "Why are you so angry when you should celebrate your victory?"

The twins, along with the other children, gave her confused looks.

Herja smiled at them all and spread her arms wide. "Think about it! You caught us. You weren't even supposed to know we were here, yet you caught us in your trap. You did a wonderful job."

Wickham didn't think it would work, but to his surprise, several children puffed out their chests.

"We did, didn't we?" Donnelly said.

"You did," Herja replied with a nod. "You have all passed the test. You used quick thinking to assess the situation and take steps to protect yourself."

Wickham nodded, making himself smile as well. He wished he knew what the adults at the camp had told them, but it didn't really matter right now, it seemed. The children accepted the praise, looking very pleased with themselves.

Rhett narrowed his eyes at Wickham but said nothing.

"Well, since you have proven yourselves, Wick and I will walk with you to the top of the mountain," Herja continued. "We won't interfere any longer."

The children seemed to accept that. It took some time, but the whole group went again. Wickham found himself near the back while Herja was at the front with his brothers. Well... he wanted to keep an eye on them. Now he could, and there was no more need to keep hidden.

If only he could get rid of this knot in his stomach saying he'd messed up...

CHAPTER
NINE

HERJA DID her best not to intervene with any of the difficulties the children faced during the rest of the day. Being in the group differed from tailing them, though; they kept looking to her to solve their problems.

She didn't exactly dislike it. It was exhausting, but she had learned how to point out what people were doing correctly and what they needed to improve on with Penelope's help. She found putting those techniques into play was very useful in this situation.

Once they reached the Silver Springs, Herja and Wickham extracted themselves from the welcoming speeches. As the children were divided up for their meal, Headmasters Twila and Valiant approached the two.

"We have a tent set up for the two of you," Headmaster Twila said. Though her expression was stern, her tone was gentle. "We've got a lot to do yet, but you should rest before we have our talk."

Herja winced. "I did tell the kings and queens we were doing this."

Headmaster Valiant nodded. "King Lantos flew up to tell us. However, regardless of it, we still have a few things to talk to you about."

"Yes, sir," Herja said meekly. She bent her head as she followed Wickham to their tent.

They were going to be in so much trouble. Even though she had only been trying to help Wickham feel better in these circumstances, she suddenly realized how it would look to the Headmasters like the two of them didn't trust anybody else to look after the children well enough.

The tent had a divider down the middle, so each side was private. Each side had a cot with blankets. Herja was grateful for the privacy as she changed into clean clothes, then lay down on the cot. After two nights of sleeping on the ground, it felt amazing.

All of her muscles were stretched and sore, more than they really ought to be. Maybe she had done something wrong with her stretches?

"Herja, can I take care of your injuries now?" Wickham asked.

Herja looked at her arms. The scratches were red, but she had already cleaned off the dried blood.

"Yes," she said anyway, knowing that Wickham would be antsy to take care of her all the same. She rolled up to sit on the cot.

Wickham rounded the partition and sat on the edge of her cot. He pulled a witch hazel mixture from his pouch and dampened a clean cloth before dabbing at her injuries.

"I'm sorry you got hurt," he said, sounding miserable.

"It's not your fault."

"It is. I'm the one who messed with that griffin baby."

Herja rolled her eyes and winced as Wickham found a cut still open. "It's not your fault. The griffin needed help. It's too bad we couldn't just explain to them that we were trying to help. The parents were defending their baby. It's nobody's fault."

Wickham moved to her other arm. "I'll feel better once everyone is back down the mountain. But with how many children there are, we'll probably wait at least two days for everyone to go through the Silver Springs."

"Three or four, most likely," Herja agreed.

The four Headmasters—Valiant, Twila, and two humans—would

take each child individually to the springs. To give that sort of individual attention to such a large group would take a lot of time.

"Do you think they'll send us back down early?" Wickham asked. He finished her arm, took her chin in his hand, and studied her face.

His touch made butterflies erupt in her stomach.

"Er.... Maybe," she said distractedly. Then she swallowed hard.

Today, watching him interact with the children made her realize there was something else they had never talked about. She still wasn't sure where they stood with each other, but if they were going to pursue a romantic sort of relationship, it was best to get the big-ticket items out of the way first... right?

"So, you like being around children, don't you?" she asked, uncertain of herself.

Wickham nodded as he dabbed witch hazel on her cheek.

"You want to have children one day, don't you? I mean, you want to be a father." Herja drew in a shaky breath as he nodded again, looking distracted. "How many children do you want?"

"I don't know. I haven't really thought about that except in vague terms." Wickham seemed to catch her expression for the first time. He lowered his hands to his lap, anxiety sparking in his lovely eyes. "Why? Do you want children?"

Herja rubbed the back of her neck, feeling awkward. "I don't know. They just seem like so much pressure. I like spending time with children sometimes, but it usually ends up overwhelming. I'm not sure I'd make a good mother."

"Maybe you just need to spend more time with children and learn how to relate to them better?" Wickham suggested.

"Or maybe this is just proof we're incompatible as a romantic couple."

Wickham was quiet as he moved to a clean spot on his cloth and dipped it in the witch hazel again. His lips tightened as he finished cleaning the injuries on her face.

A horrible feeling knotted Herja's stomach. "Please say something."

"It doesn't mean we aren't compatible."

"But if what you want and what I want are diametrically opposed, how are we supposed to be happy? One of us will end up with something we don't want," Herja said. Her voice shook, and her stomach's twisting, knotted feeling grew even worse.

Wickham folded the used cloth into his herb pouch's 'dirty' side. "You said you don't know if you want children. That means maybe you will know when you get to know them more."

"Or maybe I won't, and my uncertainty proves I shouldn't have a child," Herja countered.

"Is this a conversation you really want to have? Or do you want it to wait for a later time?" Wickham asked, looking back up at her.

Herja hesitated. Did that mean he wanted to save it for another time? "I... I don't know. I just feel like there are so many problems, and I don't know what I'm supposed to do with them," Herja finally admitted. "I don't emote well, and children are strange. What if I mess up?"

Wickham extended a hand to her, palm-up. "Can I hold your hand?"

That was another thing. Even though Herja appreciated being asked if he could hold her hand, it made her feel weird that he had to ask. Other people just slid their hands into each other's holds without it being a big deal... why was it such a song and dance for her?

"Yes," she murmured.

Wickham took her hand and squeezed it in both of his. "That's not something that we can figure out right now. I'm sure you'll be more comfortable with children once you're more familiar with them. We're sixteen—this is way too early to decide 'Yes, I will have a child.' We have lots of time to figure out our future."

Herja squeezed his hand back, liking the comfort that his physical touch gave her. "But we can't build a future together, only to have to throw it away because we've learned there are too big of differences in what we want."

"That's what dating is for."

He didn't understand her. How could they go through the commitment of dating and falling in love and think about marriage and children, only to find they weren't actually compatible at a foundational level? Herja couldn't imagine the pain that would put him through.

"We're a perfect match," Wickham continued, stroking his thumb along the back of her knuckles. "Which means whatever we go through, we can make it through together."

"Yes, we're a perfect match. But that doesn't mean we're fated to be mates in the marriage and babies sense," Herja replied. She thought again about her feelings and how she wasn't sure what they were.

Maybe what she needed was experience. It wasn't as though she'd had the chance to have dates or anything like that. Come to think of it; neither had Wickham. They had been awfully young when the stars paired them together.

Now she was seventeen, fourteen-year-olds just seemed like they were hardly more than babies.

"Maybe we should think about dating other people," she said slowly, her brow furrowed. "Just so we know."

"Know what?" Wickham asked. He sounded hurt.

Herja turned to him. He was hurt. She could see it in his eyes. She drew in a deep breath but wasn't sure what to say. "Know... what love is, I guess," she finally said.

"All right. We can think about it," Wickham said. His voice was carefully non-emotive.

And he took his hands from hers. Herja missed the warmth of his touch but didn't ask for him to come back.

"I'm sorry," she whispered.

"You can't help your feelings," he replied.

Tears pricked her eyes. No, she couldn't help her feelings. She just wished she could somehow fix this all. But how? She had no idea, not when she was still uncertain about her feelings.

CHAPTER
TEN

WICKHAM WOKE up early the next morning to help with the last-minute preparations for the children to go through the Silver Springs. Herja elected to help the cooks while he made sure the children stayed organized and entertained.

He was so busy with it all that he could almost put his discussion with Herja out of his mind...

Almost.

Once everything was in order, he waited outside the small stone building where the springs were housed. He'd escort the children to whatever camp they needed to go to, whether witch, dragon, or human.

"You look stressed," Headmaster Valiant noted close to noon. He sat on a small stone bench and gestured for Wickham to join him. "You're not in trouble for sneaking up the mountain with the children."

Wickham lifted one shoulder and let it drop. "I didn't really think I was. After all, we had permission from the kings and queens. But shouldn't you get back out there?"

"We're taking a break so the children can eat, and we can rest our old bones," Headmaster Valiant replied, stretching his legs out in front of him. "We'll have to find a different way of doing this. One hundred is too many for each to have the attention they need in one go, don't you think?"

"Herja and I were saying it seemed like it was too much," Wickham agreed with a nod. But thinking about Herja only made him remember what she'd said.

First, she said she might want a romantic relationship with him. Then, she said that she didn't even want to try and that they should just date other people. He understood she was confused and frightened by her feelings, but what was he supposed to do to help her?

"You look morose," Headmaster Valiant noted. "Want to talk about it?"

"Herja and I are having some difficulties navigating our relationship," Wickham replied, shrugging again. "But I don't think she'd want me to talk about it too much."

"I see... Well, I don't want to pry, but perhaps I can help if you tell me what's going on in broad terms?"

Wickham hesitated. He had previously talked about his relationship with Herja with his father, but Headmaster Valiant was another thing. Valiant didn't have that familial bond with either him or Herja.

On the other hand, he was also a witch mated to a dragon. Maybe he'd have insights that Wickham's father couldn't have.

"We seem to have diverging plans for the future," Wickham said carefully. "And we're not sure if those plans mean we're fundamentally incompatible for a relationship. A romantic relationship," he added, blushing. "We know we'll always be friends but... but there's a lot to figure out."

Valiant nodded. "The bond between a dragon and a witch is powerful, but not always destined to romance."

"I know. But I want it to be. I'm in love with Herja and can't imagine being with anyone else. Dating, holding hands, giggling, kissing—none of it." He shook his head, angry at the situation and, if he was honest, a bit with himself.

Herja couldn't help her feelings, but neither could he.

"The problem is that I don't want to make Herja think she has to be with me in that way just because I feel like this," Wickham continued, pressing his fingers to his temples. "So now whenever we talk about things, I don't know if I can actually say anything or if I'm putting words in her mouth to push her toward what I want."

Valiant kindly patted his back. "That is quite a conundrum."

"You said it," Wickham groaned. "I don't know how we can find a resolution to this. It seems impossible."

"Yes. But you and Herja are both bright, and you've proven time and time again that when it comes down to it, you work well together." Valiant offered him a smile. "I have great faith that, regardless of the outcome, the two of you will figure this out."

Wickham opened his mouth, then closed it again. Anything else he had to say would just be able to try to get the headmaster to resolve the problem for them. That wasn't possible.

They needed to pick everything apart and figure out what was so confusing about it.

Or maybe, overthinking would only make it worse. Perhaps they needed to stop trying to think and fix all their issues. Maybe they should just let their emotions guide them for a bit.

Soon enough, Headmaster Valiant returned to the other children, and Headmaster Twila came, bringing Donnelly with him. Wickham jumped to his feet, peering at his little brother. His hair and eyes were both still brown—human, then.

"Hiya, Wick," Donnelly said with a wave. "I'm going to the human camp—Rhett will be through soon. You can wait for him."

Wickham hadn't had the chance to say a single word, but he had to smile at this. Herja was right. The twins were itching for their independence.

Maybe if he'd been at home the last three years, it would help him understand better that they weren't little kids anymore. But they were still so little. As Donnelly headed to the human camp, though his steps were confident, Wickham felt a pang.

Maybe not too little, after all.

Rhett came shortly after with the glowing silver eyes of a dragon. Wickham grinned at him, but just like Donnelly—

"I'm going to the dragon camp. See you later, Wick." He headed off without a backward glance.

Wickham stood there for a minute, somehow both proud and disappointed. He shrugged, not wanting to deal with these confused emotions. Donnelly could have waited for Rhett, and Rhett didn't ask what Donnelly was.

Would these separate revelations push the twins apart? They'd always been so close. Now they wouldn't even go to the same school... Would they be okay when they realized that?

Only time will tell. About... well, everything.

Wickham pondered on this as he found Herja and seamlessly stepped in to help with the feast preparations. It was hard work, but by the time everything was done and night had fallen, he knew...

"I'd like to head back down the mountain now," he told Herja. He hadn't seen Rhett and Donnelly reunited at the feast, even though all the children were brought together, even the ones that hadn't gone through the Silver Springs yet.

"Now? Or tomorrow?" Herja asked him.

Wickham looked up at the darkening sky. "I guess as soon as you're comfortable."

"Are you sure?"

Wickham nodded. "I think I've learned something here. I must learn how to step back and let people figure out their problems. Sometimes it's the most help I can give."

He looked back to Herja, smiling at her. And his words sunk in deeper, making him realize this was something he had to do with her, too. She expressed confusion about her own feelings. Maybe right now, the only thing he could do was to step back and give her space to figure herself out.

Maybe it was the only thing he could do.

CHAPTER

ELEVEN

EVEN THOUGH IT WAS DARK, Herja took her dragon form to fly herself and Wickham back down the mountain. The path was full of switchbacks, meant to be an easier route for the children's shorter legs, so it wasn't that far from Mount Eldavon's peak back to the castle. It only took them a little over an hour, and for most of the way, they had winds that allowed Herja to glide.

Once they landed, Wickham took Herja's hand in his. It was a simple gesture, but she still wondered about it. Why did he sometimes have to ask, but other times she was happy he'd just hold her hand with no prompting?

Circumstances and context? she wondered, then pushed it from her mind. There'd be time for that later. She didn't want to ruin the moment right now by over-analyzing everything and getting awkward about it.

"So, do you want to see Kaia or my parents?" Wickham asked with a glance at her from the corner of his eye.

Herja's heart beat a little harder. "Um—is that a test?"

Wickham stopped. "What?"

"Well, you want to see your parents, don't you? So why are you asking me? Unless you're testing to see how I'd react?" Herja demanded. She tightened her grip on Wickham's hand so he couldn't take it away.

Wickham was quiet momentarily before saying, "Not everything is a test, Herja. I was asking because I don't have a strong preference, and I thought you might."

Herja bit her lip. "Sorry."

"You don't have to apologize. I guess we still have a lot to learn, right?" But he still looked... unhappy, and Herja wasn't sure why. He shook himself and tugged her hand. "Let's drop in with my parents first; then, maybe we can see Kaia and the others."

She nodded and let him lead her to where all the families were still camped in the courtyard. His family was just sitting around the fire with light stones hanging over their heads while David read a story to Tara.

Upon seeing them, Larissa quickly came over to embrace Wickham. "What are you doing back?"

"We got caught by Rhett and Donnelly, and they don't want us there," Wickham admitted.

Tara bounded out of David's lap. "Are Rhett and Donnelly witches like you?"

Wickham smiled at her. "We'll wait for them to get back down, so they can tell you the news themselves."

"But I don't want to wait," Tara complained.

Herja understood that—waiting was awful.

Larissa picked her up. "Oh, but we're going to have to. Wick, Herja, do you have plans, or would you like to stay to chat for a bit?"

Wickham turned to her with hopeful eyes.

Herja considered a moment before she nodded. Her neck felt oddly stiff as she did so, but she would not be any more comfortable around them if she didn't let herself get used to them.

"Can Herja read me a story?" Tara asked Wickham.

"Why don't you ask Herja, sweetie?" David chided gently.

Herja had to bite back a smile as Tara turned to her and clasped her hands just under her chin. "Will you read to me, please?"

As awkward as being around people she didn't know was, there was something extremely welcoming about being asked to read a story. Herja found a pleasant spot to sit and accepted the book that Tara handed her. It was illustrated with simple images that Herja enjoyed looking at.

They spent the evening reading, and even though Herja's voice grew tired, she still enjoyed it. So much so that when Tara sleepily asked her to spend the next day together, she agreed.

Wickham beamed at her as they left to go see Kaia and the others. "Tara likes you," he told her.

Herja blushed a little. "Oh, she enjoyed being read to."

"Yes, but she likes you, specifically."

Herja grinned to herself and walked a little taller.

The next day, Herja came back to Wickham's family camp early. She and Wickham were going to show Tara around the castle grounds, even though she'd already had a few days to explore.

"Look, it's a magpie," Tara said as they walked around the pond. She pointed to a reed where a blue, white, and black bird stood, swaying back and forth.

"That's a blue-throated warbler," Herja corrected.

Tara stomped her little foot. "No. It's a magpie."

"Magpies are bigger than that, though," Wickham said.

"It's a baby."

Herja crouched down to Tara's level and inspected the bird from her viewpoint. It did look something like a magpie. "Look at its tail. It's got a shorter tail than magpies. And baby magpies look like baby chickens. They're covered with fluffy down rather than feathers."

Tara wrinkled her nose. "It looks like a baby magpie to me."

"Sometimes things aren't what they look like, in any case. Like that," Herja pointed to a dark shape in the water. "What do you think that is?"

"A rock," Tara replied.

Herja grinned. "It's a turtle."

"No."

Herja grabbed a little stone and tossed it several feet from the turtle into the water. It dipped under the water and disappeared.

Tara gasped. "It was a turtle!"

"It was, Herja was right," Wickham said brightly. "I thought it was a rock, too."

Tara pointed at the bird. "So that's not a baby magpie, either!"

"No," Herja agreed.

Tara pointed to another bird. "What's that one?"

"It looks like a red-winged blackbird," Herja replied. "Look at how it's all black but has that splash of red on its wing? It's pretty simple, isn't it?"

"Yeah, it is," Tara replied.

The rest of the morning was filled with Tara pointing at things and demanding to know what they were. After some time, rather than just answering, Herja gave her clues and guided her to the answer.

At lunchtime, Herja was exhausted from the bundle of energy. As much as she enjoyed the questions and figuring everything out, it quickly became too much.

"I need a break," she told Wickham quietly when Tara was busy playing with a bunch of the other children. "I'll get something to eat and come back later, okay?"

"Sure," Wickham replied. "I'll get Tara back to the camp for food and meet you there. She should take a nap after food, so we'll have some time to hang out with the others."

Herja nodded—that sounded like a good plan.

She returned to her room, got food from the icebox, and then returned to bed.

As she ate, she reflected on the events of the day. Even though she had enjoyed spending the morning with Tara, sharing information and teaching her how to identify various wildlife, it was exhausting. She was just as happy now, knowing she could hand the little girl back to her parents and regulate herself again.

The problem was that children could easily become overstimulating. She wasn't sure how to handle that. Perhaps through more exposure, but she had lived with younger children at the orphanage, too. She had never really learned how to deal with them.

The door to the suite opened, and Herja pulled the curtains around her bed shut, so she wouldn't have to interact with people. She just needed some peace and quiet.

Now that she thought about it, there was a reason King Lantos hid in a closet before the opening ceremonies. As Kaia and Nolen talked about their plans for the afternoon, Herja wished she could have a closet to hide in, too, just for the quiet.

"Did you see Herja and Wickham with his little sister?" Kaia asked Nolen.

Herja tensed.

"They looked so cute," Kaia continued. "I wonder if they'll go into childcare."

"Maybe," Nolen said. "But I'm pretty sure Wickham wants to be a doctor."

"He could be a pediatrician. And Herja could be a teacher. She's good at it."

They left again, presumably with their food, and Herja let out a breath of relief. All the same, Kaia's words stuck. A teacher? She had never seen herself as a teacher... but she enjoyed figuring out ways to help her classmates when they were having trouble.

Could she deal with the high-energy needs of kids, day after day? Herja sighed. She wasn't sure she could do it.

CHAPTER
TWELVE

OVER THE NEXT FEW DAYS, Wickham did his best to stay busy while waiting for the children to come back. He and Herja spent a lot of time with Kaia, Nolen, and the others, hearing detailed stories about their time in Odentia.

Despite his attempts to find time when they could just sit and talk, Wickham found he had very little time with Herja alone. The palace was so full of people, not to mention there was so much to do.

Even more surprising was when Queen Abigail asked to speak with the two of them. She was the head of the educational branch of the government, and apparently, Headmaster Valiant had sent her a letter stating she should talk to them.

Wickham was shy and embarrassed to talk to the queen, but Herja got right down to it. She explained their thoughts about dividing the groups of children up more in the coming years so that each child had a more individual approach.

"It hasn't been a problem in the past, making sure each child got the individual attention they needed for their education and these ceremonies," Herja said, "because the groups were smaller. But we have an increasing population, and things have to change to keep up with it. Otherwise, we'll start losing them."

Queen Abigail nodded thoughtfully. "You're quite right. I've been thinking a great deal about this. We need to make sure that the Silver Springs remains accessible to everyone."

Herja nodded. "And, regarding outside of the Silver Springs, more research needs to be done into neurodivergence. So that teachers can be trained on how to best approach students who might not learn well in the traditional settings."

"Oh?" Queen Abigail said, her brow furrowed. "Why would you say that?"

"Because I'm one of them. Except all the tests I've had have come back 'uncertain' in their results, so I'm in a grey zone that doesn't receive much attention." Herja sighed heavily. "And that's caused me a lot of trouble."

"Would you like to talk to me more about it?" the queen asked.

Herja nodded, then turned to Wickham. "You can go if you want—I have a lot that I want to talk about, and I know the twins will be coming back soon."

Wickham hesitated. Yes, he wanted to be there for his brothers, but he also wanted to be here for his mate.

Herja smiled at him as though she understood the dilemma he didn't say aloud. "Go on. I'll see you later."

Wickham stood and bowed to the queen, who nodded in return. It was a relief to leave her audience chambers, even though she had been nothing but courteous to them. Would he be expected to rub elbows with kings, queens, and other government officials? He didn't see the appeal.

But he would if that was what he needed to do for Herja's career.

He returned to his family, hoping he didn't miss the twins yet. As it happened, he had. They were already there. Tara kept staring at Rhett's new silver eyes while Donnelly chatted animatedly about everything that had happened.

"I'm a balancer," he explained proudly, puffing out his chest. He looked earnestly at Wickham. "If you and Herja ever fight, you come to me, okay? I'll figure it out."

Wickham laughed as he hugged his brother. "For sure. What about you, Rhett? What was your favorite part of the trip?"

Rhett shrugged. "Catching you and Herja in my trap."

"Excuse me?" Mother asked, eyes widening.

"Yeah, we caught them in a big net," Donnelly exclaimed.

Wickham nodded once, but his attention was still on Rhett... he looked the same way Wickham had felt when he became a witch. He desperately tried to hold it in but feared what this meant for him.

"Rhett, do you want to help me get some water?" Wickham asked. Maybe if he got his brother alone, Rhett could confide in him.

"I'll come, too," Donnelly said.

Father intervened. "I need you to help me get this fire started. Wick and Rhett can go alone."

Wickham nodded once to his father, grateful that he understood the plan. Putting an arm around his little brother, Wickham led Rhett away from the family.

"You don't look very happy," Wickham noted once they were walking. "You look like you might struggle with some stuff... want to talk about it?"

Rhett shook his head. "It's a gift."

By the tremble of his voice, Wickham knew he didn't believe it all that much. "You know, when I became a witch, I was terribly disappointed. I worried about everyone, and it took me a while before I could look into a mirror because I didn't feel like myself anymore... it's okay if you wish you weren't a dragon."

A single tear rolled down Rhett's face, and he wiped it away. "It's not that. I just wish I wasn't a dragon without Donnelly. I don't think I can do it on my own."

"It's okay to feel this way. But you know, you won't be on your own. You'll have us all to help you."

"But I don't know if I can put the kingdom first." Rhett scrubbed his eyes.

Wickham nodded. "I know it's a hard thing to think about. But we are here for you, Rhett. And you don't have to figure it all out right now. That's what's so wonderful about having an entire year before you even go to the Institute."

Rhett wiped his eyes again. "I don't want to talk about this with you."

"Why not?" Shock rippled through him.

"Because you're my brother, and you don't tell me things how they are. You're always just trying to make me feel better." Rhett glared at him accusingly.

Wickham thought for a moment, then nodded. "I can understand that... if Herja was willing, would you talk to her about it?"

"Your mate?" Rhett looked uncertain.

"You could ask her, at least," Wickham suggested. "She's a dragon, too, after all. And then there's my friend Penelope; you can talk to her, too."

Rhett shrugged. "Maybe."

Rhett remained quiet while they got the water and headed back to camp... where Tara was throwing a tantrum because she didn't want to have supper and go to bed, she just wanted to go straight home.

With Tara causing a ruckus like that, Wickham could understand quite well why Herja wouldn't want to have kids. They were draining and challenging to deal with. Not everyone was built to deal with their meltdowns.

But at the same time, the two of them were only seventeen. Yeah, some people knew exactly what they wanted from their futures at seventeen. He'd known he would be in the medical profession since he was thirteen.

Kids were another matter, however. Herja didn't say she didn't want children, only that she wasn't sure she did want them—and why should they give up their opportunity to be happy together because of 'maybe's?

They shouldn't give it up. But how could he get her to understand this as well? It wasn't as easy as explaining his feelings to her because her feelings were just as valid.

How could they reach the middle ground? Where did they go from here?

CHAPTER

THIRTEEN

BY THE TIME Tara had calmed, they had eaten, and the twins were sleeping, Wickham had decided.

Herja was right when she said these issues were putting space between them. No, he couldn't be pushy, but wanting to have everything straightened out wasn't being pushy. Telling Herja that he wanted to risk having his heart broken in the future wasn't being pushy.

He had to share his truths and accept whatever came from it.

Filled with determination, he started looking for her. First, he checked with Queen Abigail to see if she was still in the audience. Herja wasn't there, so he scanned the room in the ambassadorial wing. She wasn't there.

Finally, he headed back outside. Soon, he found her sitting next to the pond, a notebook open on her lap as she scribbled rapidly in it.

"Herja," he called as he drew closer.

She looked up and smiled at him. "Hold on a minute, Wick. I just need to finish this up."

She continued writing as Wickham came to sit next to her. The moonlight glowed overhead, lighting her black hair in ways that made it glimmer a vibrant purple and green, just like the scales of her dragon.

Herja closed her notebook and looked up again. "What's up?" she asked.

And Wickham's mind went blank. Everything he'd been so sure of remained in his heart, but the words would not form. How was he supposed to tell Herja what was in his heart without words?

"Wick?" Herja frowned at him. "Is everything okay?"

"Um... I had something to ask you," he said, twitching on the spot now.

She said she wanted to try a romantic relationship with him... did that mean dating to her? Or when she said that they should date other people, was that how she actually felt? Wickham no longer knew what he was supposed to think or do here.

Herja slipped her notebook into her pocket. "Yes?"

"Rhett's upset," he blurted, latching onto the one thing he knew would be helpful. "He's uncertain about being a dragon. I tried to talk to him about how I felt about being a witch, but he told me I wouldn't understand. So, I was hoping you might talk to him."

Herja picked at her thumbnail. "Are you sure? I'm uncertain I'd be very helpful."

"I think maybe what he needs most is someone he can talk to without pressure," Wickham explained.

"I suppose it's worth a try if you think it's a good idea." Herja stood. She still looked uncertain, but a determination sparked in her eyes.

"I do," Wickham said. He offered his hand to her, and she took it.

It felt good to be able to casually hold hands like this. Wickham thought more people should do this, not tie it to dating or romance. It was just a friendly sort of thing, no pressure.

They got to the camp soon enough, and after a quick explanation, Rhett sort of listlessly agreed to talk to Herja. The two of them headed off for a walk as Wickham watched them. Now it was his turn to worry his lip between his teeth.

Despite his first impressions that Herja might not like his family, he'd realized it was just that she didn't know what to expect and was panicking over the situation.

He hoped that asking her to support his little brother emotionally wouldn't seem like he was pushing her to be around them more.

Not to mention he felt just a little bit miserable for chickening out.

"I recognize that look," Mother said mildly, coming up beside him. "Want to talk about it?"

Wickham sighed. His mother knew how to recognize when he wasn't feeling his best, which was a good thing... but sometimes he wondered if she could read his mind, making him feel a little uncomfortable in his own head.

"If you'd rather not, I can mind my own business," Mother continued. "But if you do want to talk, just let me know, okay?"

Wickham turned to her. He'd never outright told her about his difficulties with his relationship with Herja. But she knew enough. "I'm confused," he finally said.

"Confused?"

"Herja and I are deciding whether to date each other. And she said she wanted a romantic relationship, but then she was talking about dating other people. I just don't know what to think," he admitted. "And I was going to talk to her about it, but I'm afraid of what she'll say, so I didn't."

Mother's expression was soft. "Ahhh. I thought it might be something like that. So, to clarify, you're confused about what Herja actually wants, correct?"

"Yeah. And right now, it feels like potential children might split us apart before we're even together. Children! At our age." Wickham shook his head, annoyed on the one hand and incredulous on the other.

Mother sat near the fire and patted the chair next to her. "At your age or not, if you're planning on spending the rest of your lives together as a couple, the matter of children has to be decided on some level."

Wickham slumped into his chair. "But I want to have kids someday, not anytime soon, and Herja doesn't know if she doesn't want kids. So that will not be resolved."

"And what if she decides she doesn't want to have children? Is that a deal breaker for you?"

Wickham weighed her words. A deal breaker. He tried to imagine himself never being a father. It made his heart hurt... but when he thought about possible nieces and nephews, it hurt a little less.

Then, he thought about volunteering with children... even in the small village he grew up in, various community members hosted plenty of activities for the children. There were ways he could help nurture children without being a father himself.

"You've got a good heart, Wick," Mother continued. "And I want you to have everything you want. But sometimes, we have wants so opposed that we can't have them all. Sometimes, we have to pick the ones that are most important to us."

"I already know what's most important," Wickham murmured. "I just don't know how I'm going to tell Herja that without sounding like I'm pressuring her... or rather, without pressuring her. She doesn't want to hurt me, Mother. And I'm afraid I'll put her in a position where she has to."

"And that's a difficult position for both of you," Mother agreed.

Wickham nodded. "So, what should I do? I can't just keep pretending like nothing is happening. She said it's putting distance between us, and she's right. But I'm also afraid that if we decide not to date, it'll just push us further apart. Or if we do start dating and find out, we're not actually compatible—"

"Wickham." Mother lifted a hand, smiling still.

He fell silent, staring at her with pleading eyes. Once upon a time, he thought his parents could solve any problem he had.

Then when he realized they couldn't... well, maybe that was when he thought it was his responsibility to solve everything they couldn't. But he couldn't, either. Even if he wasn't a witch, even if he had never left home, there were problems bigger than all of them.

Mother hugged him. "Be open-hearted with her. Tell her the truth and work together to figure out what you need to do."

"So, blurt it out and hope for the best?" he asked doubtfully.

Mother laughed. "If that's what you have to do? Then yes."

Wickham groaned. That didn't sound like much of a plan. But he supposed it was the only one he had.

CHAPTER

FOURTEEN

THE MOON HUNG low in the sky, casting long shadows over the lush garden. Herja breathed in the sweet scent of flowers as she and Rhett strolled along the cobblestone path. Now that they were walking, she found it peaceful and was loathed to break the silence.

Perhaps Rhett was feeling the same calming effects. His hitched shoulders lowered slowly, so Herja guessed he felt more comfortable.

"So, Wickham told me you're feeling uncertain about your place as a dragon. Is there anything in particular about it you're uncomfortable with?" Herja asked, keeping her eyes straight ahead.

"Everything," Rhett muttered.

Herja nodded. That was quite a reasonable answer, she thought. More than one student in her year had been disappointed in what they'd been revealed as at the Silver Springs, while she knew of many humans who had likewise been disappointed.

"All right. Can you name one specific thing? If it helps, I can go first with something that bothered me when I learned I was a dragon."

Rhett bobbed his head once.

"I had trouble with the emphasis on the physical over the intellectual," Herja said. "I still do, to an extent. I've pushed myself hard to get stronger physically, but most of the time, I'd rather read than work out."

Rhett seemed to consider her words. In a small voice he said, "I'm a selfish person. I don't want to serve the kingdom. I don't want people to look to me for defense at all. I want to be a hermit."

"Oh, the wise old hermit job. That's a good one," Herja said, nodding.

Rhett gave her a startled look. "Huh?"

"You know, in the stories, there's always the wise old hermit living at the top of this mountain or in the belly of that jungle to give the hero sage unintelligible advice," Herja said, smirking at him. "Someone has to take it."

A smile tugged on Rhett's lips.

"There are ways to defend people without physically putting yourself in the path of what's endangering them," Herja continued, her mind racing. What sort of jobs included hermitage and defense? "Do you know that there are people who do live up in the mountains, calculating any cracks in the rock face and keeping track of weather patterns in case of rockslides?"

"They do?" Rhett stood a little straighter.

"They do. Or you could be a workhorse. I imagine a dragon could till a field much more efficiently with our claws and bulk."

"I don't think dragons are allowed to do that," Rhett said doubtfully.

Herja took a moment to process that. Yes, that was a problem Eldavon faced. There were high pressures for witches and dragons to fall into specific roles... Not that anyone was forced to take those jobs, but even without force, societal pressure still existed.

"The thing about Eldavon is that we're always learning and growing," she said slowly.

Rhett wrinkled his nose. "What does that have to do with anything?"

Herja gestured at a bench to sit on, then took her own seat. "Many times, I feel like I don't fit in. Not just as a dragon, but also as a person. It's hard to deal with. I feel like maybe there's something wrong that I don't have a place or purpose in the kingdom."

"That's what I feel like. I don't have a place as a dragon."

"And that is a failing of our society. I'm not saying we should just give up on society, mind you," Herja said quickly. "Or even that the surrounding people are failing. Just that sometimes we're built differently, and that's not a bad thing."

Rhett scrubbed his nose hard. "If it's not a bad thing... then why does it feel bad?"

Herja shook her head. "Because... well, because Eldavon is growing, and there is always that awkward phase or uncomfortable stages with growth. Do you know how lobsters grow?"

"Now you're talking about lobsters!" Rhett threw his hands into the air. "I don't understand you. I don't understand one bit."

Herja couldn't help but laugh. "I am jumping around a lot, aren't I?"

"You are."

"But this is for a reason, I promise. Lobsters have a hard shell, and when they get too big for that shell, they have to shed it. That means struggling to break free, which can be a very long and painful process. But once they are free, they're vulnerable until their new shell hardens."

Rhett nodded slowly. "So... what you're saying is that Eldavon has outgrown its old shell?"

"Getting close to it, at least. Which means we're getting to the point where we as a society will be breaking free of it, and during the learning process of where we want to be next, we will be off-balance, uncertain." Herja sighed as she thought of her conversation with Queen Abigail.

Yes, Eldavon was changing. And that was a good thing since they were now learning how to help vulnerable people who weren't built for the societal norms that had been struck in previous generations. Those norms may have protected Eldavon's society in the past...

But they were getting too big for that.

Just like me. I'm changing and growing. This means I have to shed my old shells so that I can continue to grow...

Especially with Wickham. He'd been so patient with her already.

She couldn't keep dancing around, keeping him at arm's length because one day she might hurt him or be hurt herself.

It's time to be vulnerable.

"I think I understand what you mean," Rhett said, returning her attention to him. "But I'm still unsure how it helps me if I'm not good enough to be a dragon."

"Oh, but you are good enough," Herja replied. "And you're going to be part of splitting the old shell and building a new one. Regardless of where your dragon takes you. Whether you become a hermit or a king, every person gives Eldavon something unique."

Rhett got to his feet. "Thank you, Herja."

"I hope you feel better."

He grinned and hugged her. "I do. Thanks."

Herja hugged him back. "Can you get back to your camp alone?"

"Yup. Bye!"

Rhett skipped off, his shoulders thrown back, clearly feeling more confident.

Herja moved off the bench to a grassy hill. There, under the glow of a light stone, she pulled her notebook out and wrote down the analogy she'd shared with Rhett—something she could use to help herself in the future.

She wasn't sure how long she'd been there, writing before Wickham's voice interrupted her.

"Herja?"

She looked up.

"We need to talk."

CHAPTER
FIFTEEN

THE LOOK on Wickham's face made her heart beat harder. Herja attempted to keep herself calm, not wanting to read too much into it. He leaned forward slightly, his dark eyes intense on her. Her throat went dry. Was he going to kiss her?

Wickham pulled back, turning his head away. "Er... okay, so I had this all figured out in my head, but I'm going just to blurt it out. Kids or no kids, I don't want to date anyone but you. If the choice were between being your husband someday and being a father someday, I'd pick you. Every time."

Herja's chest filled with a fluttering sort of warmth. Her cheeks burned as she blushed, even as a pleased smile spread over her face.

"I don't want to choose a lifetime of having a division between us just because at seventeen, I want kids, and you might not. That's not what a deal breaker is to me. Maybe I'll change my mind about wanting to be a father—children are hard to deal with."

Relief washed over Herja... so she wasn't the only one who thought so.

"They're messy and self-centered and unreasonable." He took a deep breath and looked up at her, his expression earnest. "I can find other ways to fulfill the need to care for little ones."

"I don't want you to give up your dreams for me," Herja replied.

"I know. Just like I don't want you to give up your dreams for me... but the thing is, sometimes we have to pick the better dream. And I don't want your choice of whether to be with me to be based on a question that we won't have answer to for years."

Herja swallowed hard, her nerves jangling. That was true. She didn't know if she would want kids, and it could take a very long time to figure it out.

Just like she was growing increasingly unsure about her future career path, if she decided she didn't want to be queen one day, she didn't need to base her life around that possibility. On the other hand, if she overcame these doubts and went back to it... she could also damage her chances by pretending it didn't matter.

"And what if I want to be queen one day? You don't want to be the king."

"No," Wickham agreed. "But the kings and queens don't have to be married couples."

"But they always are."

Wickham shook his head. "Not always—you should know that."

Herja opened her mouth and shut it again. That was true. Most of the time, the dragon, witch kings, and queens were mated to each other, just as the humans were married, but it wasn't always the case.

"My life in politics will overwhelm yours, though, even if you don't become a king," she pointed out, unwilling to let it slide. She didn't want Wickham to make plans based on unrealistic dreams...

"And I'll deal with it."

Herja stroked the spine of her notebook, thinking. If she just let herself react to Wickham's words, they filled her with giddiness for which she didn't have a name.

Or rather, she did have a name for it. Love... but she wasn't sure it was the true sort, the kind that would last forever. Her fingers moved to the pages of her notebook. It wasn't like what she thought it would be. It wasn't this rush of realization; it didn't take her breath away every time Wickham looked at her.

No. It was something even deeper. He was *safe*. He was *home*. And she couldn't imagine her life without him.

She looked up, tears pricking her eyes. But they were happy tears as she beamed at him. "Ten years."

Wickham's brow furrowed.

"When we're twenty-six, we should have graduated from whatever secondary education we decide to go for. We'll be in a better position to know ourselves better."

"Ten years. Yeah, that sounds reasonable." Wickham nodded, looking relieved. "So, does that mean... we can start dating?"

"Yes. As long as you're okay with it being long distance after we graduate from the Institute," Herja said.

Wickham's shoulders slumped. "What do you mean? I can go anywhere you need to be."

"Except the best medical school is here in the capitol," Herja replied, shaking her head. "And while I'm still not certain where I will go, I'll most likely be moving around quite a bit. I'm looking into becoming an educator. But no single school will teach me everything I want to know. I'm going to have to make my own course. Which means moving around."

She opened her notebook, where she had been writing the various possibilities. "Like I said, I don't know for sure. But right now, this is what I think will be the best one."

She shared the brief research she had already done, explaining how she planned to use her 'grey area' diagnosis to work with other children who were not quite neurodivergent and not quite neurotypical.

"This way, I can work with children and teach them, as well as with adults, and still have my personal space to retreat to," she finished as she shut her notebook. "I don't know if it will work, but that's the goal right now."

Wickham nodded, picking at the grass. "And I can't really work it out to move to different medical schools. As long as we have different places to go for secondary education, we won't be physically together."

Herja shook her head. "No, we won't. But that might be for the best, anyway. If we got married and lived together, we might find that certain choices regarding kids would be made for us."

A startled look came to Wickham's eyes. "You want to get married?"

"Not until we're twenty-six," Herja corrected. "And only if we both want to at that time."

"I think I can live with that timeframe," Wickham murmured. He sat up a little straighter as a light came to his eyes. "You know, Kassandra always told me that medical school was super intense and that she left to become a herbalist because she didn't have the time to spend with her family while training."

"I've heard that, too," Herja agreed.

"So, it will be better for us to be long distance. That way, I won't feel like I'm neglecting you." Wickham burst out laughing—Herja wasn't entirely sure what was amusing, but she smiled as well.

She really did like the sound of his laughter.

Wickham flopped back on the grass, grinning up at the sky. "There's so much we can do once we're graduated. We could travel around for your research or find a central location to settle down like Kaia's parents."

Herja lay down next to him, curling on her side. The future was terrifying in the sense that nothing was certain. A singular event could destroy the best of plans.

Adoption, diagnosis, it was all so uncertain. Herja didn't like uncertainty. She wanted everything laid out before her to know exactly what her next step would be. Some things just couldn't be sure.

But there was one thing she was absolutely sure about—a future with Wickham was filled with hope.

"We could work with Queen Abigail and King Sydney to arrange exchange students so that other kingdoms could benefit from Eldavon's knowledge... and we in Eldavon could benefit from their knowledge, too," she said.

"We could open an orphanage—maybe," Wickham said. "Although that would bring the same problems with being biological parents. Being overstimulated by the noise and needs of kids."

Herja nodded, though she found the idea of being a caretaker less intimidating than being someone's mother.

"You could be a caretaker, and I could be a janitor," Herja giggled. "I don't need to have a fancy education after all."

Wickham laughed with her and tucked his hands behind his head. "Oh, that's true. The possibilities are endless."

Herja rolled closer. "Wickham?"

"Yeah?"

She took a deep breath, steeling herself. "Will you kiss me?"

Wickham smiled. He leaned in, stroking her hair from her face. He kissed her gently, and Herja found it easy to figure out how to kiss back, so long as she wasn't overthinking it. The kiss didn't last long, but when he was done, they both were grinning.

Herja rested her forehead against her perfect match, her fated mate. Oh, yes. The possibilities, indeed, were endless.

The End

If you enjoyed this book, consider leaving a review on Goodreads, Bookbub, or your favorite retailer.
Reviews help me reach new readers.

Read *The Quest for the Kraken's Ink*, the third book in the *Defenders of the Realm series!*

Join my newsletter at www.mhlebeault.com for writing updates, sneak peaks, review copies, sales, and giveaways!

www.ingramcontent.com/pod-product-compliance
Lightning Source LLC
Chambersburg PA
CBHW020644130626
46552CB00003B/1386